伊姆蘭的診所

卡蒂·蒂格

IMRAN'S CLINIC

KATI TEAGUE

叢書編輯：羅斯瑪麗·蘭寧

Series Editor : Rosemary Lanning

Magi Publications, London

Published in 1991 by Magi Publications,
in association with Star Books International, 55 Crowland Avenue, Hayes, Middx UB3 4JP

Printed and bound in Hong Kong.

Translated into Chinese by Chinatech
ISBN 1 85430 211 6

伊姆蘭說：" 傑伊，該起牀了。媽媽說，今天我們要帶你去診所。"

"Time to get up, Jay," said Imran. "Mum says we're taking you to the clinic today."

伊姆蘭問：" 媽媽，爲什麼傑伊要去診所？他病了嗎？ "

"Why does Jay have to go to the clinic, Mum?" asked Imran.
"Is he sick?"

媽媽回答說：＂他沒有病，他要去打針。所有的孩子都要打針，你像他這麼大時也打針。＂

"No, he needs an injection," said Mum. "All babies have injections. You had them when you were his age."

有很多人在等着看醫生。伊姆蘭說：" 傑伊，別着急，
快輪到你了。"

There were lots of people waiting to see the doctor. "Don't worry,
Jay," said Imran. "It will be your turn soon."

這時，安娜走了進來。伊姆蘭問她想不想過來看傑伊
稱體重。

Then Anna came in. Imran asked if she'd like to come and watch
Jay being weighed.

伊姆蘭說："傑伊長重了。"護士說："是的，他長得很好。好，我想醫生現在可以看他了。"

"Jay *is* getting heavy," said Imran. "Yes, he's doing very well," said the nurse. "Now, I think the doctor is ready to see him."

他們走進醫生診室時，醫生問：" 這是不是傑維德？"
伊姆蘭說：" 是的，我們叫他傑伊，他是我弟弟。"

"This is Javed, isn't it," said the doctor as they went into her room.
"Yes, but we call him Jay," said Imran. "He's my brother."

醫生給傑伊打了一針。伊姆蘭焦急地問道："他痛不痛？"
醫生告訴他："只痛一會兒，打針能幫他防止生病。"

The doctor gave Jay an injection. "Does that hurt him?" asked Imran anxiously. "Only for a moment," said the doctor, "and it will help him not to get sick."

安娜的爸爸邀請伊姆蘭到他們家來。他說蓋爾和利亞姆
也要來。

Anna's Dad invited Imran to come back to their house. He said
Gail and Liam would be coming there too.

在蓋爾和利亞姆來到安娜家時，伊姆蘭把去診所的事都講給他們聽，他說："我們也辦一個診所好嗎？"

When Gail and Liam arrived, Imran told them all about the visit to the clinic. "Shall we play clinics?" he said.

大家都喜歡這個主意，他們跑進安娜的房間。
伊姆蘭說："我要當醫生。深呼吸。"

They all liked the idea and rushed into Anna's room. "I'm going to be the doctor," said Imran. "Take a deep breath."

安娜說：" 現在來給嬰兒稱體重，
我的嬰兒比你的嬰兒重。"

"Now let's weigh the babies," said Anna. "Mine's much heavier than yours."

他們把所有的玩具都拿出來，在洗澡間的秤上稱一稱。

They got out all the toys and weighed them on the
bathroom scales.

蓋爾說：" 這隻小熊受傷了，需要用繃帶包紮一下。"
說着，她就撕下幾張廁紙。

"This teddy has hurt himself. He needs a bandage," said Gail,
unrolling some toilet paper.

利亞姆問：" 誰要打針？ " 伊姆蘭說：" 我不打！ "

"Who wants an injection?" asked Liam. "Not me!" said Imran.

安娜說：" 我給這隻小熊喂點藥。"
她沒注意到她灑了很多水。

"I'm giving this teddy some medicine," said Anna. She didn't notice how much water she was spilling.

蓋爾給大多數的動物玩具進行了包紮，她正在設法包紮
自己。她說：「天啊，我被絞纏住了。」

Gail had bandaged most of the animals, and was trying to
bandage herself. "Oh dear, I am getting tangled up," she said.

正在這時，安娜的媽媽進來了。當她看到他們把房間弄得
亂七八糟時，非常生氣。

Just then, Anna's Mum came in. She was very cross when she saw
what a mess they had made.

她說：" 現在你們要把東西整理一下！"

"Now you can tidy all this up," she said.

他們整理得很賣力，不一會兒就把所有的東西都收拾好了。

They worked very hard and soon everything was cleared away.

安娜的媽媽說：" 這樣好多了，診所應是很整潔的。
你們現在想吃點什麼嗎？"

"That's better," said Anna's Mum. "Clinics are supposed to be tidy.
Would you like something to eat now?"

正當他們吃東西時，伊姆蘭的媽媽來接他。

While they were having their snack, Imran's Mum arrived to collect him.

伊姆蘭說：" 媽媽，我們開了個診所。" 媽媽笑笑說：
" 我知道。但我聽說它比我們帶傑伊去的那個診所亂得多。"

"We made our own clinic, Mum," said Imran. Mum smiled.
"I know," she said. "But I heard it was a lot untidier than the one
we took Jay to!"

睡覺前，伊姆蘭去向傑伊道晚安，對他說：
"診所遊戲真好玩，我想，我長大了要當醫生。"

At bedtime, Imran went to say goodnight to Jay. "Clinics are fun. I think I'll be a doctor when I grow up," he told him.

Playbooks

Picture books   23 x 20cm, 32 pages

Imran's Clinic
Imran's baby brother needs his injections, so after a visit to the real doctor, Imran and the others set about creating their own surgery in Anna's bedroom!

Liam's Day Out
Liam's parents take the four youngsters on a visit to a farm. Being an urban child, Liam is rather apprehensive at first, but he soon finds things to enjoy in the countryside.

Anna Goes to School
It is time for Anna to start school, and she's not too keen, but after her first day there, she's ready for more.

Gail's Birthday
Mum and Dad and baby brother, Jack, all contribute to the fun on Gail's special day.

These titles are available in English only and in the following dual-language editions (with English): Bengali, Chinese, Greek, Gujarati, Hindi, Punjabi, Turkish, Urdu, Vietnamese.

Board books   15 x 15cm, 12 pages

Getting Dressed
Shows how and how not to do it.

Faces
Including happy, clean, dirty and masked ones.

Opposites
Near and far, sweet and sour, and others.

Arms & Legs
How they help us play and run.

'Delightful books which will certainly encourage the young child to behave as a reader.'   *School Librarian*

'These books offer excellent opportunities for learning and conversation in company with an adult.'   *Contact (PPA Magazine)*

These titles are available in English only and French only and in the following dual-language editions (with English): Armenian, Bengali, Chinese, Estonian, French, German, Gujarati, Hebrew, Hindi, Hungarian, Italian, Japanese, Latvian, Lithuanian, Polish, Portuguese, Punjabi, Spanish, Ukrainian, Urdu, Vietnamese.

Best-selling Magi dual-language picture books

Naughty Bini   Mamta Bhatia and Keir Wickenham

Happy Birthday Bini   Mamta Bhatia and Anna Louise

Grandmother's Tale   Moy McCrory and Eleni Michael

A Country Far Away   Nigel Gray and Philippe Dupasquier

Purnima's Parrot   Feroza Mathieson and Anna Louise

Sometimes . . .   Anna Louise

The Boy Who Cried Wolf   Tony Ross

Anita and the Magician   Swaran Chandan and Keir Wickenham

A Brother for Celia   Maria Martinez i Vendrell and Roser Capdevila

After Dark   Maria Martinez i Vendrell and Roser Capdevila

Ben's Baby   Michael Foreman

Mum's Strike   Marieluise Ritter, Leonard Ritter and Leon Piesowocki

Amar's Last Wish   Parvez Akhtar and Keir Wickenham

Brush and Chase   Eileen Cadman and Keir Wickenham

The Eagle that Would not Fly   James Aggrey and Wolf Erlbruch

Hello Bump   (Flap book)   Christopher James and Steve Augarde

Bump Sings a Song   (Flap book)   Christopher James and Steve Augarde

Bump in the Park   (Flap book)   Christopher James and Steve Augarde

Bump at the Beach   (Flap book)   Christopher James and Steve Augarde

Bump is Busy   (Board book)   Christopher James and Steve Augarde

Look at Bump   (Board book)   Christopher James and Steve Augarde

Here is Bump   (Board book)   Christopher James and Steve Augarde

Bump at Play   (Board book)   Christopher James and Steve Augarde

All these Magi dual-language books are available in English only and in Bengali, Gujarati, Hindi, Punjabi and Urdu with English. Some titles are also available in Chinese, Greek and Vietnamese with English.